ON
GUARD

# bOUnCE

# ON
# GUARD

PATRICK JONES

darbycreek
MINNEAPOLIS

Darby Creek
A division of Lerner Publishing Group, Inc.
241 First Avenue North
Minneapolis, MN 55401  USA

For reading levels and more information, look up this title at
www.lernerbooks.com.

Front cover: © pzAxe/Shutterstock.com, Susan Rouleau-Fienhage (background).

Main body text set in Janson Text LT Std 12/17.5.
Typeface provided by Adobe Systems.


**Library of Congress Cataloging-in-Publication Data**

Names: Jones, Patrick, 1961- author.
Title: On guard / by Patrick Jones.
Description: Minneapolis : Darby Creek, [2017] | Series: Bounce | Summary: "She is the star player on her basketball team, until her sister is injured in a violent crime. Instantly, her game is derailed, and she becomes a second victim. Can she save her scholarship season?"— Provided by publisher.
Identifiers: LCCN 2015044802 (print) | LCCN 2016012796 (ebook) | ISBN 9781512411232 (lb : alk. paper) | ISBN 9781512412079 (pb : alk. paper) | ISBN 9781512411348 (eb pdf)
Subjects: | CYAC: Basketball—Fiction. | Sisters--Fiction. | Grief—Fiction.
Classification: LCC PZ7.J7242 On 2017 (print) | LCC PZ7.J7242 (ebook) | DDC [Fic]—dc23

LC record available at http://lccn.loc.gov/2015044802

Manufactured in the United States of America
1-39638-21281-3/18/2016

Thanks to the fab five of Sarah, Christine, Bhargavi, Amber, and Megan

Mercedes Morgan's shot exploded like a bullet: fast, accurate, and painful to her enemy.

"Three!" the point guard, Cheryl, yelled in delight. The other starters of the Birmingham North Wildcats team—Halle, Toni, and A.J.—followed with slaps and bumps.

Mercedes didn't acknowledge her teammates, the shot, or the score. To do so meant removing her "don't mess with me" game face, letting down her guard, and rejoicing about something small. It was three points. The first of many she figured she'd score in her senior year.

Back on defense, Mercedes kept her left

arm outstretched in front, waiting for her chance to swat the ball from the Hoover guard. The Hoover guard cut left, but Mercedes hung tight. She closed off all good options and forced a bad pass. The other team would score, that was a given, but Mercedes didn't want any to come from her zone. She owned it like gangs owned blocks back in her old neighborhood.

Before the second quarter, Coach Johnson told the other players to feed Mercedes the ball. "She's hotter than Alabama in August," Coach said.

As Mercedes walked toward the locker at the end of the half, she took inventory of the sparsely populated bleachers. Jade? Yes! Mom? Yes, always. Dad? No, working, also always. Little brother, Lincoln? Yes, but not happy about it. Big sister, Callie? Never.

Mercedes knew where Callie would be, but she tried to block the image like she rejected shots. Callie never sat in the stands. She stood on a corner in their old neighborhood. There Callie dealt in danger, always on guard, not knowing when her number would come up. *Not if*, Mercedes thought, *but when.*

**2**

"Wait up!" Jade yelled as she raced toward Mercedes, her thickness weighed down with multiple rings, bracelets, and necklaces. Everything about jiggling Jade made Mercedes smile.

Cheryl gently poked Mercedes's side. Mercedes had been elbowed so many times on the court that her taut stomach absorbed the blow. "Jade's so all about you," Cheryl said in words barely audible through her laughter. The rest of the Wildcat starting five agreed. They were gathered around Mercedes's locker as they were every school morning.

"I don't have time for Jade during the

season." Mercedes checked the schedule on her cell. School. Practice. Study. Family. Mercedes knew she'd only be able to give Jade the time she deserved if a genius invented a longer day, but that didn't seem possible.

"You lie," Halle said. Mercedes's embarrassed face didn't deny it.

When Mercedes turned to leave, Cheryl latched onto her arm, holding her in place until Jade arrived. Almost a foot shorter than Mercedes, Jade sometimes made Mercedes feel like a giraffe in the hallway, unlike the gazelle she resembled on the court.

"Sorry I'm late," Jade said, catching her breath. Mercedes waited for her to give a reason, but Jade just removed her backward Barons ball cap and tossed it into the overstuffed locker that they shared. Jade unloaded her bag and took out the books for her morning classes. Both she and Mercedes held AP Calculus texts.

Mercedes tried not to be suspicious as she watched Jade. She loved the silver "Love" necklace that hung around Jade's neck.

Mercedes had given her the necklace on their one-year anniversary. She hated the green "Loyalty" tattoo Jade had inked on her left arm before they'd met—it looked a lot like the one that Callie wore with pride. Mercedes wondered if Lincoln hid one under his long sleeves.

"See you after practice?" Mercedes asked softly, trying not to flinch. Getting a shot blocked on the court was a bad feeling, but having Jade say no to her for any reason was worse.

"Always," Jade said before she kissed Mercedes on her strawberry-gloss lips. "Forever."

**3**

"You see the story in the paper?" Coach Johnson asked Mercedes at the end of a hard practice. Mercedes thought Coach pushed them more after they won than after they lost. Since they were on a four-game winning streak, each practice seemed worse than military basic training.

"What story?" Mercedes asked, fighting a yawn. She'd been up until eleven texting with Jade, past one studying, and until two worrying about Callie. Callie had studied nothing since she dropped out at sixteen and jumped into the life of working for Robert, slinging back in their old neighborhood—what

Mercedes just called *the life*. Some nights Callie came around the house, but mostly she stayed at Robert's place. Mercedes didn't know which was worse.

Coach showed Mercedes a printed story from al.com about the first few weeks of high school basketball. It wasn't a long story. Nobody in Alabama cares about basketball until the college football season ends and the Crimson Tide secures the national championship.

"Am I the only Wildcat?" Mercedes asked. The attention embarrassed her at times, especially in front of her teammates. *It isn't my fault*, Mercedes thought, *that I'm this good.* Yes, it was practice and hard work, all those little bottles of character traits that coaches sell, but Mercedes knew better. Like LeBron in basketball or the Williams sisters in tennis, some people became rulers of the court because of God-given natural ability. "I mean, didn't the story mention Cheryl or Halle?"

Coach pursed her thin lips. "This means there'll be college recruiters. I want them to talk to me first. You okay with that?"

Mercedes frowned. "Do I have to talk to them?" Mercedes's small voice belied her five-foot, eleven-inch frame.

"Do whatever you want," Coach said.

*Easy for you to say*, Mercedes thought. Mercedes imagined herself in college. Then she saw her sister on the street. Mercedes heard the cheers of a packed field house, and then she heard the tears of her crowded church.

"Mercedes?"

"Thing is, Coach," Mercedes said, staring at her well-worn Nikes, "I don't know what I want."

"Is anybody home?" Mercedes called into the darkness of her house. She guessed her dad was still at work, while Wednesday night her Mom attended church. "Lincoln, let's eat!"

Mercedes dropped her bags by the front door and headed into the kitchen. She opened the fridge and pulled out leftover chicken stir-fry and the makings of a salad. Judging by the amount left, Lincoln probably hadn't eaten yet. She hoped he was absorbed in video games with his goofy friends like in junior high, but those goofs never came over anymore. He had new friends that she didn't like.

"Lincoln, let's eat!" Mercedes pounded hard on his door. Nothing. "Lincoln, let's go!"

The door opened. Lincoln glared at his sister. She'd noticed he'd been doing more of that recently, and he was participating in family time less and less. "What do you want?" he snapped.

"Less attitude," Mercedes snapped back, earning another glare. "You hungry?"

"I'm good." Mercedes glanced over her brother's shoulder. She saw an open pizza box. She smelled the garlic, but something else too. Even with the window open, the odor lingered. She heard a cough and saw Joel, one of Lincoln's new friends, on the floor. He wore expensive shoes.

"Don't let Mom or Dad catch you," Mercedes said. "I won't snitch you out, but—"

"You're right about that." Lincoln's once-cute smile curled into an in-your-face smirk.

Mercedes took a step back as if to size up her younger and much smaller brother. She sighed hard. "What's wrong with you? Don't you see Callie—"

Lincoln started rapping about money, but Mercedes couldn't place the song. She wished he studied more and wasted less time with Joel. Lincoln used to be a good student, but high school had come down hard. He'd dropped out of football and refused to go out for basketball.

"What are you up to?" Mercedes inspected him head to toe: new shoes on his feet and that smirk on his face. Their family had left their bad neighborhood, but Lincoln had brought it with him.

"Kat, what's the record?" Mercedes asked during her team's last time out. They were ahead by a wide margin. Coach had left Mercedes in, not so much to pile on points as to make a milestone.

The team manager, Kat, searched her phone. Coach scowled at the sight, but a thin smile emerged when Kat broke the news. "The record for the most three-pointers in an Alabama girls' game is ten." Mercedes and her coach exchanged glances like co-conspirators of a bank heist.

"Up to you," Coach said. Mercedes wiped a towel over her short hair. "You have eight."

Mercedes glanced at the clock. Four minutes left. Making two more threes against the smaller and slower Bessemer team was a slam dunk. "Kat, what's the *real* record?"

Kat didn't need to ask what she meant. "The record is fifteen threes in a boys' game."

"Look, up there." Coach pointed at three women, overdressed for a high school gym. Each held a phone in one hand and, Mercedes suspected, her future in the other. Scouts.

"If I shoot too much, they'll think I'm a selfish player," Mercedes worried aloud. Her teammates disagreed, Cheryl the loudest. "What do you think, Cheryl?" Mercedes asked.

"You get open, you'll get the ball." They fist-bumped as they ran onto the court.

Mercedes cut toward the basket, took the pass, tossed back to Halle, then raced herself behind the three-point line. Left fake, right sprint. Pass. Ball in hand. Shoot the hoop. Three. The Bessemer team inbounded and tried pushing the ball up quickly, but turned it over right into Mercedes's hands: hands that launched a three-pointer to tie the record. The Bessemer crowd booed.

As the final seconds clicked down, the Wildcats passed to Mercedes when she got open. If she beat the double, she got the three. If she got shut off, she passed off and tried to get free. *If only life was so easy*, Mercedes thought. With seconds left, Mercedes launched her last shot. The cheering crowd drowned out the clanging of the orange ball off the front of the silver rim as the shot missed.

"Don't you ever get tired?" Jade sat cross-legged on a picnic table, sipping an oversize Coke and listening to music. She never took her eyes off Mercedes shooting threes in the twilight.

Mercedes launched another nothing-but-net shot as her answer. Unlike parks in her old neighborhood, this court had a net. This park felt safe. She didn't need to be always on guard.

"You were amazing the other night," Jade said.

"You mean during the game or after?" Mercedes asked.

Jade laughed and almost shot Coke out of her nose. Jade's laugh, more than her smile, figure, street smarts, or carefree personality, was what attracted Mercedes to her like a magnet.

"Watch this," Mercedes said. "I'll not only hit ten shots in a row, but I'll do it so the ball bounces right back to me. You wanna bet?" Mercedes knew there was no way in the old playground courts, where her dad first taught her to play, that she could make such a bet. Like the streets around that park, there were too many hazards to send a ball, or a life, far off course.

Jade laughed again, but then turned her jeans pockets inside out. "I got nothing to bet."

Mercedes kissed Jade, then whispered, "I'll think of something." Mercedes dribbled the ball onto the court, found the three-point line she'd marked off, and made the first shot.

"Nine more to go!" Jade clapped and started the countdown. Just as Mercedes had said, her shots sailed through the net, then bounced back to her. Eight. Seven. Six. Five. Four.

"Mercedes!" Mercedes turned toward the voice. Callie. Holding the ball so tight she thought she might crush it, Mercedes didn't reply as her older sister came closer. Callie didn't acknowledge Jade or introduce Mercedes to her entourage. "Lil sis, you *still* playing games?"

The sweat on Mercedes's forehead chilled at her sister's tone. Her blood froze solid when she saw Robert's ring-filled hand clasp hard onto her sister's shoulder. Not a touch between equals, more like an owner guiding his dog. "How you doing, Mercedes?" Robert asked. Mercedes shivered.

"What do you want?" Mercedes asked the pavement below, avoiding all eye contact, especially with the youngest-looking member of the group. It was Lincoln's new friend, Joel.

"We were rollin' by and saw you," Callie said, sounding casual. Callie tried to engage Mercedes, asking about Christmas and such, but Mercedes wouldn't speak to her. The more silent Mercedes became, the louder Callie got, finally shouting, "What's wrong with you, girl?"

Mercedes clenched her fists until she felt

Jade's arms wrap around her waist, making her feel safe. "Whatever, we're out," Callie snorted. Callie retreated with Robert and the others as quickly as she had arrived. Mercedes watched as the group climbed back into a big black SUV.

"You okay?" Jade whispered into Mercedes's left ear. Mercedes pulled away from Jade. She retrieved the ball and hurled it hard into the backboard. The ball bounced far out of Mercedes's reach. *Just like my sister,* Mercedes thought.

"Let's go," Mercedes said. She jogged toward the loose ball. "We need to study."

"Only way out of here," Jade said. "Well, for me. For you—" Jade pointed at the ball.

Mercedes ignored the ball and touched Jade's shoulders. "I don't want to leave you, ever."

Mercedes's soft words were interrupted by a loud sound and lights. Sirens. The flashing lights triggered flashbacks to her old neighborhood. She knew what life might have been if she hadn't found her passion for getting a game. Then there was her sister's passion for

The Game. Both had risks, both held rewards. On the court, Mercedes's hands went high to gather a rebound. In the distance, Mercedes saw Callie's hands held high over her head, then behind her back. As the police pushed Callie into the squad car, she turned her back, but Mercedes felt like she was the one turning her back on her sister. She'd get up and out because of her skills, while Callie's choices could only leave her down and in jail, or worse, six feet in the ground.

The back of the team bus, where Mercedes normally sat firing off jokes, seemed louder than normal, and the trip to play rival South High for an away game seemed longer than usual.

Mercedes sat by herself, music booming in her earbuds, then coursing through her veins like blood, as she scrolled through pictures of her family. Mom. Dad. Callie. Her. Lincoln. Family.

Callie and Mercedes were three years apart. Mercedes marveled at how much she looked, dressed, and acted like her sister for so many years, and how quickly things had started to change. In junior high, Mercedes mastered the court, at the same time Callie made her first appearance in juvenile court. Not her last. Photo by photo, sisters became strangers: Mercedes, who once did everything she could to follow in her sister's footsteps, sprinted in the other direction. Her sister's tight white beaters, expensive shoes, and letters on her skin were a polar opposite to Mercedes's colorful polos, court-ready kicks, and proud letters on her report cards. Around tenth grade, Callie's smile died.

Mercedes wondered about her sister's mug shot. The arrest Mercedes witnessed wouldn't result in juvenile time. Callie was twenty, yet she clung to her old friends, habits, and haunts.

Cheryl tapped Mercedes on the shoulder. Mercedes popped the bud out of her left ear.

"Everything okay?"

Mercedes hesitated. She didn't open up to just anyone. Cheryl was just a teammate, not a soul mate like Jade.

"Is it about your sister?" Cheryl asked.

*Did everyone on the team bus know?* Mercedes wondered. Maybe she wasn't avoiding them;

maybe they were avoiding her. "I'm sorry to hear."

"Don't worry about me," Mercedes said, trying to sound confident. "I got game."

"If I was you, I'd be more worried about your sister than a game, but that's me." Cheryl frowned. "Maybe because I pass and don't shoot, I always worry about the other person first. But you do what you gotta do. You've got enough pressure anyway with all those scouts buzzing."

Mercedes wanted to put the bud in, turn up the music, and collapse into the beat. What if there was a story in the paper about her sister getting arrested? What if the scouts connected the two of them? The bass boomed along with Mercedes's pounding heart. *What if?*

"I'll take care of you." Cheryl slapped Mercedes softly on the shoulder and then left her alone. Mercedes faked a smile, whispered a "thank you," and started scrolling through photos again.

Mercedes glanced at her phone to see another missed call from her mom. In just over an hour, Mercedes would put on the maroon North jersey she wore with pride. But in the morning, she'd wait in a line for over an hour at County to see her sister wearing an orange uniform of shame. She called Jade instead of her mom.

"Jade, this is Robert's fault," Mercedes said as soon as Jade picked up. Jade listened as Mercedes retold the story of Callie getting mixed up with Robert. "He's a dead weight around her ankle."

"Mercy, staying in the life was her choice," Jade whispered. "Like leaving it was mine."

Mercedes said nothing as the bus pulled up to a light. Green. Yellow. Red. So easy, but life didn't give such easy directions. The only one that made sense was yellow: use caution.

"You okay?" Jade interrupted Mercedes's thoughts. Mercedes didn't answer; she scrolled photos, past her sister whom she couldn't help. She stopped on one of Lincoln from last year. He was smiling, not smirking. Mercedes frowned. Was he following Callie's path?

"I'll be okay." Mercedes took a deep breath. In just over an hour, she'd be on the court for all thirty-two minutes if she got her way. In those thirty-two minutes, nothing mattered except an orange sphere like the sun. Her life revolved around basketball, especially when the rest of life spun like a loose ball out of her control. "Don't worry about me, Jade, I'm okay."

"But you're not okay." Jade's soft voice dropped softer than even a whisper. "I love you so much, Mercy. That's why I hate it when you lie to me."

"I'm blowing it!" Mercedes kicked over a trash can in the visiting locker room. Kat followed behind and picked up the spilled garbage, muttering a torrent of filthy language.

"That's enough!" Coach shouted, but Mercedes heard nothing but sirens in her head.

Unable to swear, Mercedes smashed her fists hard into the old tan lockers. The sound bounced around the tiny room like thunder. "Cheryl, don't you *ever* pass me the ball again!"

Cheryl started to speak, but Mercedes shouted over her. "Anybody but me!" She turned to Kat, snatched the clipboard out of her hands, and ripped up into tiny pieces the score sheet for the game that showed her line: zero for eight from the field, including three missed threes.

Instead of handing the clipboard back to Kat, Mercedes punted it across the room. When she did, Coach bounded across the room and grabbed Mercedes's left arm.

"Let go of me!"

Coach clutched Mercedes's arm tighter and dragged her into the shower. With one hand, Coach pressed against Mercedes's chest to hold her in place, and with the other, she turned on the water. "You'd better cool down, now!"

Mercedes stood in the cold water, shivering, the water masking her falling tears. It was a game with scouts in the stands and they had to win, but she'd lost her rhythm. Mercedes wondered if she'd lost her soft shooting touch when the police locked the hard cuffs on Callie's wrists.

Back in the locker room, she heard Coach trying to fire everyone up even as ice raced through Mercedes's veins. She reached up and turned off the water. Kat stood a few feet away and tossed her a towel. Mercedes stripped off her clothes and wrung the water out of them. She squeezed as hard as she could—her hurting hands aching with the effort—to get her clothes dry.

"You ready to play?" Coach asked. Mercedes wrapped the towel tight around her. Kat picked up Mercedes's clothes and took them into the other room. Mercedes heard the hand dryer turn on loud.

"I want to," Mercedes said, her voice hoarse from tears. "I don't know if I can."

"If you want to change your behavior, then you can. It's that simple."

From the gym, Mercedes heard the roar of the crowd as the South High team returned to the court. "You can go, Coach. I'll be okay." Mercedes shivered again.

"Tell me what's going on." Coach leaned closer and put her hand on Mercedes's shoulder.

"No." *My sister is locked up*, Mercedes thought, *and my brother's out with the wrong people.*

Coach shook her head. "Mercedes, I'm here for you, and so are your teammates."

Mercedes stared at the shower floor. "Don't you need to get out there and coach?"

"That's what I am doing," Coach said. Kat returned with Mercedes's damp clothes and tossed them to her. "Kat, the team's yours until I get back. Like always, do your best."

Kat, all five-foot-one of her, sprinted off toward the gym as if a starter pistol had just fired. "Mercedes, get dressed and then come see me." Mercedes did like she always did: followed her coach's orders.

After Mercedes returned in her damp clothes, Coach said, "Tell me. It will help." Coach motioned for Mercedes to sit by her on the bench. A bench made for quick changes, not for long stories like the one Mercedes told about her sister. How despite the surroundings they grew up in, Callie seemed on the right course until the dark cloud called Robert stormed into her life.

"When I'm on the bus and it stops at a traffic light, I can't stop thinking about Callie standing on the corner with Robert's hand on her shoulder pushing her down."

Coach started to speak, but stopped. Mercedes sensed Coach wanted her to say more.

"I don't know what to do," Mercedes confessed. "I've got to change what she's doing."

Coach patted Mercedes again on her shoulder. "Let me show you something." Coach dipped her left hand into her maroon North polo and pulled out a necklace. "You see this, Mercedes?"

The thin necklace held a large pendant with lots of writing. Mercedes stared hard and read aloud the words engraved on it: "God, grant me the serenity to accept the things I cannot change, the courage to change the things I can, and the wisdom to know the difference."

"What you can change is yourself. Focus on your game, not your sister's." Coach pointed at the gym. "I know one thing that you can change. I know you *can* change the score of this game!"

With her uniform still cold and damp, Mercedes felt her game was ready to heat up.

"I don't want you talking to any college recruiters without us around," Mercedes's mom said. Her father quickly agreed, but it was hard for Mercedes to take their stern tone to heart. Between her buzzer-beating three—clinching North's come-from-behind victory over rival South—and Callie getting released from jail, Mercedes felt as if two Christmas gifts had arrived four days early.

"Coach said the same thing," Mercedes said as she leaned against the refrigerator.

"You want me to screen the calls?" Lincoln asked. "I'll act as your agent. Now, listen here, my big sister wants two first-class tickets, one for me and another for her. Now—"

"That's enough, Jerry Maguire," Mom said as she placed the meatloaf on the table.

"Who is that?" Lincoln asked. Mercedes laughed at how loudly her mom sighed. Lincoln crossed his arms and mumbled under his breath, "Don't bust me like that again, Mom."

At the word "bust," the smile that had been on her mom's face since Callie got out of jail vanished. Mercedes's mom wasn't alone in hoping Callie's release might be a turning point. Mercedes had called Callie and left a message, inviting her to the Spartans' Christmas Classic, a tournament Mercedes knew her team would win. But Callie hadn't called back.

"Why was everyone laughing at me?" Lincoln asked, his tenth-grade voice cracking. Unlike tall Mercedes, Lincoln was an undersized bully target. He'd need someone to protect him, and Joel wasn't the answer. *If I go away to college*, Mercedes thought, *who will stand guard over Lincoln?* Going away to school would be the best thing for her, Mercedes knew. Yet when she thought about everyone she'd leave behind, it seemed like the worst option. Her dad worked too much and her mom worried too much, so Mercedes felt that keeping Lincoln on the right path fell on her. Just as she was on her team, in her family she was on point, always on guard.

"Is Jade coming over for Christmas dinner?" her mom asked. Before Mercedes could answer, the phone in the kitchen rang. Her mom wiped her hands on her apron and picked up.

"Hello?" Mercedes's mom said into the phone, her voice so soft. A softness in contrast to the hard sound her mom's body made as it crashed onto the kitchen floor seconds later.

## 10

"Is she going to be okay?" Mercedes asked her parents. Their mouths moved about as much as Callie's eyes: not at all. Mercedes couldn't see her sister's mouth; it was hidden by a complicated apparatus to help her breathe. Other machines performed other functions. A day ago, her sister had been flesh and blood, but with one bullet, Callie had become part robot.

"Mom, answer me." The beeping and hissing of machines served as her mom's answer.

"I'm calling Jade," Mercedes said, but her mother shook her head forcefully.

"You're needed here." Her mom reached out to touch her, but Mercedes backed away.

Mercedes stared at her sister in the hospital bed. *She looks so small*, Mercedes thought, *like a thin tree branch surrounded by a big white cloud.* "What can I do?" Mercedes asked.

"Pray," her parents said at the same time. Mercedes wondered where Pastor Curtis was. He was one of the first people her dad had called after he helped Mercedes's mom off the floor and spoke with the police. Where was he? Or the doctors? Or anyone who could help Callie?

"I'm worried about Lincoln," Mercedes whispered. "We should have told him the whole truth, not just that she got shot, but that she might never—"

"He doesn't need to know that now." Mercedes's dad rose from the chair where he'd been sitting vigil for hours. "Anyway, once she's better—"

"They said she's not going to get better," Mercedes said through tears. Her mother began to cry with her. Mercedes's dad wrapped his long arms around the two of them, squeezing.

He held tight until the door opened. "How is she?" asked a tall man in a brown suit. Mercedes shook her head, not really answering. Mercedes couldn't say aloud what she knew inside. Callie would never get better. She could not change it; she must accept it.

The man handed her a card.

"Detective Lloyd Wheeler, Birmingham Police," the card said. Under his contact info, the words "to protect and serve" mocked Mercedes, who knew she had done neither for her sister.

**11**

"How is she?" Coach sat down next to Mercedes on the bus to the holiday tournament. She wasn't the only one concerned. Rumors had spread like airborne pathogens among North students. Mercedes heard genuine concern in Coach's voice, but she felt numb, maybe like her sister felt, if she felt anything at all. Another two days had passed—another triumph of machines over death.

Mercedes couldn't answer or even make eye contact. She stared at the ugly green seat of the old schoolbus. The engine sputtered as the bus stayed parked, waiting for other players.

"Is there anything I can do?" Coach's voice

floated into her ear, but when Mercedes felt her coach's familiar hand on her shoulder, she knocked them off like they were fire.

"Don't touch me!" Mercedes shouted. Coach started to talk, but Mercedes drowned her out by banging her fists hard against the smudged window. "Stay away from me or else!"

Mercedes turned and stared at Coach but it wasn't Coach's face she saw; it was Callie's face, eyes closed yet somehow seeming to stare up at her from that hospital bed. In her pocket, Mercedes's phone buzzed, each ring a lightning bolt. Another well-wisher, another "is there anything I can do?" When Mercedes saw big-mouth Cheryl climb on the bus, she crawled over Coach, rushed past Cheryl, and sprinted into the parking lot. The cold December wind chilled her burning face and eyes. She stood motionless, her hand over her eyes, wishing she was blind. In the distance, she heard hushed conversations as her teammates boarded the bus. Then, she heard a voice nearby.

"It's up to you." Coach talked as softly as Mercedes had ever heard. "It's just a game."

Mercedes stayed silent, so silent that when the driver honked the horn, she felt as if she'd jumped out of her skin. Every noise, loud or soft, near or far, made her jump. "I can't."

"Take all the time you need," Coach said, but the words barely registered. Mercedes dialed Jade. As she waited for Jade to answer, Mercedes yawned. Like a full-court press, her nightmares had shut down her sleep. Mercedes, who felt fearless on the court, found herself scared to close her eyes, afraid of the bad dreams sure to come.

**12**

Jade's car barely fit the definition. Patched and re-patched, the small green Dart was older than Jade. Hardly anybody had working cars back in Mercedes's old neighborhood. "Climb in, Mercedes," Jade said.

They had talked and texted, but it was the first time Mercedes had seen Jade since Callie's shooting. Mercedes wondered if Callie's shooting would be a dividing line in her own life: the time before and the time after. But with Callie in a coma, Mercedes felt time stood still. Callie was a broken stoplight: no yellow, red, or green. "Mercy, you doing okay since—?" Jade asked.

Mercedes clutched onto the door but hesitated, stuck on Jade's unfinished question and on the inevitability of what had happened. Her mom kept saying that Callie getting shot made no sense, but Mercedes knew enough of the streets to know that her mother was wrong. She suspected her dad knew too, but neither said a word. "Mercy?"

The cold wind shot through her. Mercedes pulled her blue and white Atlanta Dream hoodie tighter but couldn't make her feet move. The door handle dug into her skin like a knife.

Mercedes heard the driver's-side door open and Jade's tiny sneakers smack against the pavement, the sounds made louder by the empty parking lot. Mercedes wondered if her teammates on the bus were laughing and busting each other like always, or were they quiet, worrying about Mercedes? Did they even care about her? Was she just a three-point machine?

"Mercy, can you get in the car?" Jade whispered with the same fragile tone she had on the phone, the same tone it seemed everybody used to speak to her lately. Mercedes felt Jade's hand fall gently on her shoulder as it had a hundred times before. Mercedes waited for the warm tingling she always felt, but instead a burning sensation overcame her. She jerked away from Jade.

Mercedes collapsed onto the ground in tears.

"Mercy?" Jade whispered, but Mercedes couldn't respond. Every ounce of energy served her worry, her sorrow, but also her memory. Images of Callie flashed through her mind, setting off a memory tug-of-war. Every time Mercedes recalled her sister laughing, the sound quickly became replaced by the beeping machines and hospital clatter. Every image of her smile fell victim to the image of the complicated medical devices keeping Callie alive.

"What can I do?" Jade whispered as she reached out and grabbed Mercedes's hands to help her up. Mercedes batted Jade's arms away like they were two pythons primed to crush her.

"Don't touch me!" Mercedes leapt to her feet, but Jade grabbed onto her. Mercedes fought against her, but Jade just held on tighter until Mercedes collapsed into her arms. Slowly, Jade helped Mercedes get seated in the car and strapped the seat belt across her. When the seat belt clicked, Mercedes startled. Wasn't that the same sound as a trigger being pulled?

"Where to?" Jade asked, but Mercedes didn't answer. She pressed her face against the glass, watching the buildings pass by like something out of a movie. *It's not a movie*, Mercedes thought, *or a dream. It's a real-life nightmare*. Just like the ones she continued to have almost every night. Images of bullets and dead bodies haunted her nights like ghosts.

When they arrived at Mercedes's house, Jade parked against the curb. "What are all those cars?" Jade asked Mercedes as she looked through the cracked windshield. Mercedes knew the answer.

"People with questions," Mercedes said, her jaw set tight. "Get me out of here."

"Where do you want to go?" Jade pushed down on the gas and began driving.

Mercedes paused and then dug her hand like claws into the car seat. "I want to see *it*."

Jade pressed down her long black hair. "It?"

Mercedes pulled at the frayed fabric of the Dart. "The corner where Callie was shot."

Jade stopped the car, shook her head, and drove fast in the opposite direction.

**13**

Mercedes felt odd standing on the court, as if she wasn't one of the team. Apart.

Everybody spoke to her in whispers, like Callie getting shot was some kind of secret. But after Jade had showed her the article on al.com, Mercedes guessed that everybody knew the story. Nine other players filled out the court, but as Mercedes stood at the three-point line, she felt alone. The Lamar High guard in front of her was as good as invisible. She dribbled and launched her normal shot, but the ball hit Cheryl in the back, falling far short of the basket.

"What the f—" Cheryl started, but stopped

when she saw it was Mercedes who had taken the shot. Before, Cheryl would've busted her, but instead she said nothing. Mercedes wondered if her teammates really thought she was that fragile, that she might break if they said anything. It seemed everybody in her life had forgotten how to speak. Words came hard, sentences harder. Maybe, Mercedes thought, because all her family had was questions: Who? Why? But mostly, when?

When would Callie wake up? When would Callie live again? When would Callie die?

The only people with more questions than her family, it seemed, were the police. Maybe they sensed Robert or one of his crew had pulled the trigger. Callie was insignificant to them, but Robert was big game whose head the cops would love to nail on their wall. They swarmed like bees, buzzing her and her parents' phones until they all blocked the number.

"Mercedes, heads up!" Cheryl yelled and passed the ball back to her. There was nothing but silence, as if the gym were a sound vacuum. Just ball against floor. Three times.

Mercedes launched the shot. Her feet off the floor and the ball in the air, Mercedes waited for the space to fill with hope and possibility, but there were only question marks.

Who? Why? When? When would Callie wake up? Questions clouded her court vision.

It took the loud sound of her missed three banging hard against the backboard to clear her vision. Instead of playing her position, Mercedes raced toward the net. Cheryl inhaled the rebound and passed to Halle. Halle shot a brick from the baseline. Under the basket, Mercedes leapt into the fray, elbows flying, intent on violence. The ref's whistles sounded like sirens.

"Play smart!" Coach shouted at Mercedes to start the second half. Mercedes wondered why Coach didn't leave her on the bench where she belonged. She'd had four shots, four misses, two turnovers, one foul, and zero confidence. She couldn't block out the noise of the crowd or the noise in her head.

Halle grabbed the ball from the jump and passed to Cheryl, who dribbled down the court and called the play. Mercedes stared at the court, not her teammates. An unfamiliar voice inside herself was growing louder: *Please don't throw it to me!*

Cheryl passed to Halle, then set a pick. Mercedes trudged into position. The Lamar guard raced toward her, but it was too late. Mercedes held as the clock ticked down. She looked to pass, but no one was open. Dribble. Stop. Look. Pray. Shoot. Miss. Not just the net, but also the rim: an air ball filled with iron.

"No worries," Cheryl yelled. Mercedes stared at the scoreboard. Down ten points, but the answer to her team winning was to be down one person. Her. Mercedes hustled into position. She set herself. The hometown favorite Lamar High guard faked left, moved right. Mercedes stared at the empty real estate in front of her and listened as the ball tapped off the backboard for an easy two.

The buzzer sounded as subs jogged onto the court. Mercedes saw no one coming to replace her. She tried to get Coach's attention but failed. Up in the stands were scouts, but that was about the future. Mercedes lived suspended in the present with Callie.

With Mercedes not a threat, Lamar double-teamed Cheryl, forcing a turnover. Two more points. Ball back up the court. The guard backed off, daring Mercedes to shoot and miss.

Jump. Shoot. Miss. Cheers. No buzzer, but no matter. Mercedes sprinted for the bench.

"You okay?" It was Cheryl. While North had
won the game despite Mercedes, the bus ride
back had been silent. Mercedes was surprised
by Cheryl's call the next morning. "Mercedes,
talk to me." Mercedes said nothing until Cheryl
pressed hard, just like she did on defense.

"No, I'm not all right." The contents of
Mercedes's broken heart, nervous mind, and
wounded spirit spilled out.

Cheryl kept quiet until Mercedes heard
words she'd never heard from a teammate.
Words she'd said to others, yet that no one
but Jade had said to her before. "Mercedes, it's
okay. Don't cry."

Mercedes took a deep breath like she was trying to pull the tears back into her eyes. "It's too much," Mercedes said.

"If there's anything we can do," Cheryl offered. Mercedes mumbled and hung up the phone just as she heard the back door open. There stood her parents, sweating even in December.

"What are you doing?" They should have been at the hospital.

Her parents looked at each other, but not at Mercedes. Her mom held a bucket in one hand and a brush in the other; her dad held two brushes. Her mom emptied the bucket into the sink, then filled it with water. Her dad washed his hands under steaming water and bubbling soap. Mercedes walked toward the sink and saw the white surface turn scarlet as her father cleaned off his hands.

Mercedes followed them back outside. Her dad slammed the door. It was good that Lincoln was at Grandma Bee's house, she thought, so he could avoid all the anger. Her parents walked with slumped shoulders toward the garage where the word "SNITCH" had been spray-painted in red letters two feet high on the garage door. A word stronger than muscle, soap, and water.

Mercedes had her why. Callie's shooting wasn't random; it was revenge.

"Mercedes, what is your problem?" Coach said, drawing stares from the rest of Mercedes's teammates. Coach never called out a player during halftime. But North was eight points behind a smaller, less skilled Carver High team at the half. It was just one game, but in a single-elimination tourney, one loss was all it took to go home. A place Mercedes didn't want to be. Part of her wanted to be on the court, but Coach had Mercedes parked on the bench.

"I didn't tell you to sit down," Coach said. Mercedes stood like a cadet at basic training waiting to be screamed at, humiliated. All deserved.

"You want to play in the second half?" Coach asked in a challenging but not angry tone.

"I don't know." Mercedes had never answered anything but "yes" to that question.

"Kat, give me the ball bag!" Coach shouted. Kat tossed the white mesh bag at Coach.

Coach tossed the ball bag toward Mercedes, who let it fall at her feet. "Pick it up!"

Mercedes complied as Coach grasped her end of the bag. "You want to play?" Coach pulled her end of the bag hard. The tough fibers dug into Mercedes's hands but she hung on. "So your sister got shot. So you don't think you can play. So everything is a struggle!" The louder Coach yelled, the harder she pulled. The harder she pulled, Mercedes yanked back even harder. The friction of the bag against her skin caused a burning sensation. Her hand was on fire, yet she would not, could not, let go.

"Maybe you're a loser like your sister! Maybe you belong on that corner!" Coach yelled.

Mercedes gritted her teeth; she felt her muscles tighten like steel cable as she pulled. "You can't play because you're struggling. The struggle weighs you down. Let it be, Mercedes."

Coach tugged hard on the bag; Mercedes yanked back harder. "Let it be, Mercedes!"

Mercedes yelped, released the bag, and crumpled to her knees.

"What do you want, Mercedes?"

"Coach." Mercedes rose from her knees and stood tall, her torn-up palms open for all to see. "I want the ball."

"That was one of the most impressive second halves I've seen in all my years," a tall woman with short, graying hair told Mercedes as she stood by the team bus.

"What?" Mercedes shouted, startled by the stranger. She leaned against the bus for safety.

"Do you have a minute?" the woman asked. Who was she? A scout? A cop? *Those jobs have a lot in common,* Mercedes thought. *Old people with power judging young kids, deciding if they are "good" or "bad," with the answer determining their future.* Mercedes wondered if a gray area existed anywhere in the world.

"I'm Tina Franklin, Auburn." Mercedes

swallowed her smile. Auburn was only one hundred miles away, but the orange and blue Tigers seemed light-years away from her life in Birmingham.

"Have you talked to Coach?"

The woman smiled but didn't answer her question. "I saw what kind of athlete you are, so tell me, what kind of student are you?"

Mercedes's report card was a hive of Bs, except in math, where an A stood tall. Mercedes rattled off her good grades, but the Auburn envoy cut her off with a smile.

"I didn't ask about your grades," she said. "I asked, what kind of student are you?"

*One that doesn't like quizzes or trick questions*, Mercedes thought. Behind her, she heard teammates on the bus celebrating the win thanks to Mercedes's twenty points in the second half.

"At Auburn, student athletes are students first and athletes second." The woman reached out her hand. "If you can graduate college, you can play. That's how it works at Auburn."

Mercedes took the card and buried it in

the pocket of her Dream hoodie, which seemed right. "Thanks."

"You played like two different people out there," the Auburn recruiter observed.

Mercedes agreed but didn't tell her why. She'd just begun to understand it herself. If Callie was a broken stoplight, then Mercedes was stuck at a crossroads, not knowing what to do.

"God, grant me the serenity to accept the things I cannot change, the courage to change the things I can, and the wisdom to know the difference," Mercedes said under her breath. The whizzing of machines and blaring of alarms throughout the hospital covered up the noise of her prayers. Mercedes stared at her sleeping sister.

"I cannot change this." Mercedes held her sister's limp hand. "I must accept it."

Mercedes looked at her own left palm where she could still see the marks left by the rough mesh bag. "I must accept this," she repeated in time with the breathing machine.

Mercedes released her sister's hand and knelt down by the bed. She said the serenity prayer over and over, each time louder until her voice reached that of Coach calling a play or Pastor Curtis trumpeting out a prayer. She knew from the doctors that no prayers would be answered: Callie wouldn't wake up. But as she thought about her sister's life the past few years, Mercedes knew that the Callie she loved had died years earlier.

Mercedes stood, took a deep breath, and pulled down the sheet covering her sister's motionless body. Staring at the "Loyalty" tattoo and other gang tats, Mercedes knew she needed the courage to change Lincoln, or help him change, if he was traveling down the dark path that she suspected. Mercedes would need to do more than talk. She would need to act, to be a leader.

Mercedes ran her left hand along the length of her own unmarked right arm. She didn't totally blame her sister for wanting to belong to something bigger than herself, something that gave her life meaning. Her team did that; Jade did that.

"I cannot change this," Mercedes whispered. "I must accept it."

Taking one last deep breath, Mercedes lifted Callie's hands so they rested against Mercedes's chest and she imagined their hearts beating in time together. "I must let it be."

**19**

"Play your game!" Coach shouted at Mercedes as the fourth quarter ticked down. Game she had—twenty points: five threes, two layups, and one foul shot. She loved playing on the road; it was something about making the opposing crowd hate you and then breaking them. Pleasant Grove, the host of the tournament, had, as always, found themselves in the final game against North.

"You got this?" Cheryl asked. Mercedes smiled in reply. She looked into the crowded stands to see her family, which included Jade. They'd left the hospital to see Mercedes in action. Mercedes knew she couldn't let them down. If she was really going to "let it be," she'd need to focus on the present, not the past. She didn't see the Auburn scout in the stands, but she forced the future and past out of her mind.

"Play your game!" Coach yelled to the team. Mercedes felt the words in her bones.

Game. Total game. That's what Coach had taught her. She could always pass, shoot, and run faster than anyone. That's all that mattered on the playgrounds. But in college, Mercedes knew a player couldn't be one-dimensional. Sure, you could come off the bench, make some threes, but that meant you were a specialist. Not a real player, an athlete, a leader.

"Yes!" Coach shouted as Mercedes reached out, tipped the pass, stole the ball, and dribbled like a demon as they'd practiced a hundred times. This wasn't playing; it was Mercedes's muscles and mind remembering what to do when. Perfect pass. Assist. Two more North points.

Despite Mercedes playing tight D and scoring when she got a clear shot, Pleasant

Grove kept the game close. In the lead by one with five seconds left, Coach called a safe play. A.J. inbounded but Cheryl couldn't pass. About to be fouled, Cheryl passed to Mercedes. With no pass, Mercedes ducked the swarming D and hurled the ball toward the net like an orange comet. As she shot, Mercedes tumbled to the floor and was deafened by boos from the hometown crowd and cheers from her team, who grabbed their phones to catch a falling star in motion.

**20**

Mercedes and Jade sat holding hands on a big green sofa in the corner of Halle's basement. Music boomed around them, punctuated with laugher. The sounds of victory.

On the table in the middle of the crowded room sat the Pleasant Grove Girls High School Tournament trophy. One by one, Kat snapped photos of each player hugging and kissing the trophy.

"I want you up there with me," Mercedes whispered into Jade's ear.

"I didn't do anything." Jade pulled Mercedes closer. "Seriously?"

"I thought I'd lost everything, but you

helped me find my way," Mercedes said. She knew before the end of the season she needed to share the same words with Coach.

"You always had it." Jade squeezed Mercedes's hand. "Sometimes life gets blurry. That's how I was before I met you, Mercy. Everything was blurry, like looking through a haze of smoke."

Mercedes glanced at her phone, wondering if she wanted it to ring. Would it clear the haze from her life, not just for thirty-two minutes on the court, but for the rest of her days? *"Mercedes, get to the hospital quick,"* she imagined her mom's words, *"because Callie is—"* But then she didn't know which word would come next: Awake? Dying? Dead?

"So what's next?" Mercedes asked Jade. "You should apply to Auburn. I am so in."

Jade rolled her big brown eyes. "I can't get into Auburn. You know that."

While Jade had brought her grades up, Mercedes knew Jade's first two years were nothing but tough Ds. Mercedes pulled the scout's card out of her pocket. "What's that?"

Mercedes told Jade about the scout speaking with her. "You have to go," Jade said.

Mercedes rested her head on Jade's shoulder. "What about us?"

Jade didn't answer.

For all the clatter of the day's victory, Mercedes knew her future held so much loss.

"He's been banging stuff since he got home,"
Mercedes told her mom. Even though they
had tried to keep the hopelessness of Callie's
condition from Lincoln, he'd found out and
was angry. "Maybe it will make him think
twice about getting into trouble, traveling that
road, and—"

"He's not going to do that," her mom
snapped. They sat at the kitchen table.
Mercedes's father had exhausted all his vacation
time and returned to work. Her mom would
need to return to her job after the new year,
just like Mercedes would go back to school
every day, not just game days. Mercedes forced

down the thought of Callie alone, surrounded not by family, but by machines.

"You don't know what it is like to—" Mercedes started, but her mom cut her off again.

"That's why we moved here, to get you away from those influences," her mom said.

"Mom, there are corners everywhere!" Mercedes thought about the corner where Callie was shot. Mercedes knew she could never "let it be" like Coach said until she visited the scene.

"Not at Auburn," her mom said. The scout had invited Mercedes and her parents to dinner. "I'm not letting them buy you or this family. If she wants to meet us, she can do it here."

Mercedes glanced into the living room at the family photos with Callie in the picture. What if the recruiter asked about Callie? What if she knew? "I want Jade to be here. And Coach too."

Her mom sighed. "Well, I guess I have a lot of cooking to do!" Mercedes laughed.

"You need any help?" Mercedes asked.

"I do, so get your brother down here. We won't let this *thing* break us."

Mercedes said nothing. *Thing. It.* Her parents always used impersonal words like they were afraid to speak the truth, although she knew they were right. It would not destroy them. Like falling behind in a game, challenges brought people together, made them strong like a rock. Because a rock didn't bleed, it didn't cry; it smashed the scissors that would cut a life in half.

**22**

Mercedes tried not to startle when people started to hug her during the first day back at school after the holiday break. When they touched her, Mercedes backed away like they carried the plague. Some congratulated her on the championship while others offered sympathy about her sister. A few did both, which Mercedes had a hard time handling. How could she accept congratulations and feel happy when her sister lay in a coma feeling nothing?

By the end of the day, Mercedes stood at her locker, as exhausted as if she'd run a hundred wind sprints. She didn't know if she could face another day hurtling between the highs and lows.

"You okay?" Mercedes shivered at the touch on her shoulder. Jade. "Sorry, I didn't mean to scare you." Mercedes turned and pulled Jade close to her.

"I can't stop it." Mercedes still couldn't stop being startled awake by nightmares either.

"It takes time," Jade said. "It's called trauma. It just takes time and—"

"Letting it be." Mercedes stared at her palms. The marks were gone, but the image remained.

"I'm going with you to Auburn. I talked to my counselor. It's a long shot, but—"

"I'm good at long shots!" Mercedes said. Jade's laughter lifted her spirit. "You know, right now, Jade, I feel like I'm on the top of the mountain. But there's a problem with that."

"What's that, love?" Jade tugged at the silver necklace around her neck.

"You see," Mercedes started, but then stuttered like she did back in grade school. "You see how far there is to fall." Mercedes fell into Jade's arms, and Jade wrapped her in a hug.

"You'd better get to practice," Jade whispered. Mercedes wiped away tears, pulled her bag out of her locker, kissed Jade goodbye, and started toward the gym.

At the gym door stood not her coach or teammates, but Lloyd Webber, Birmingham Police Detective.

"We need to talk," Webber said, his words pushing Mercedes down the mountain.

"Could I have more potatoes?" Tina Franklin asked Mercedes's mom, who gladly passed the special scalloped potato, cheese, and chive dish. "These are delicious. I'd ask for the recipe, Mrs. Morgan, but being a college recruiter means I'm always on the road. I'm a Burger King queen!"

Everybody except Lincoln laughed. Mercedes sensed that Franklin already liked her game but also wanted to like her as a person. This dinner was a test.

"Very strong team this year, Coach Johnson," Franklin said, no stranger to polite behavior. "Will you win state?"

Coach nodded but said nothing. Maybe Coach was more used to fancy meals from recruiters rather than a homemade meal in a small house.

"We will," Mercedes said with pride.

"That's the kind of confidence you'll need to achieve good grades and then graduate," Franklin said. Then she launched into a short speech, probably canned but Mercedes didn't care, about the values Auburn looked for in a student athlete—that's the term she always used. "There are plenty of girls who can hit a three-pointer. We want girls who can study, who can—"

"Why don't you quit all this jiving and get to the bottom line," Lincoln said and pushed his full plate of food to the side. He'd been pushing his family aside too: meals unattended, homework neglected, and curfews broken. "Let's talk money and a ride."

Jade squeezed Mercedes's hand under the table, then whispered, "What's he doing?"

Mercedes said nothing.

"Everybody knows that's how the game is

played," Lincoln said as he sat up in his chair. Mercedes noticed the swagger in his voice. "Anybody who doesn't play it is a loser."

"Lincoln, that's enough!" Mercedes's dad snapped.

Lincoln rose from the table, picked up his plate, and hurled it against the wall over the sink. "That's garbage, just like all of you."

"She's not there," Mercedes told Coach just before heading out onto the court. *She* was the Auburn recruiter who left immediately after Lincoln's scene and hadn't been in touch since.

"Play your game, Mercedes," Coach said. "That's what matters. Just let it be, let it be!"

As she walked onto the court with the other starters, Mercedes glanced into the stands. Only Jade waved. Her parents were back at Callie's bedside, and she hadn't seen Lincoln since his outburst. Her parents had reported him missing, but the police only seemed interested in getting information on Callie's shooting and the people Callie had been hanging around with. From the second she saw "SNITCH" painted in red on the garage door, Mercedes guessed the shooting was Robert's doing, but she couldn't risk leaving her parents to deal with another daughter in the hospital or maybe in the grave. After declining to answer any of Detective Webber's questions at school, she'd tossed the detective's business card out with the rest of the trash.

"Let's win!" Halle yelled before the jump ball. The ball came to Mercedes, who made a quick pass to Cheryl. Cheryl moved the ball up court and called the play. Everybody got quickly into position with Mercedes cutting to the far left. Cheryl passed to Mercedes, who set for the shot, drawing the double team to allow Cheryl to break for the basket. A quick pass from Mercedes to Cheryl, then a quicker one to Halle. She slammed home the first two to wild cheers.

Play after play, North executed Coach's design like they'd practiced. When a set play got shut down, the pass went out to Mercedes, who nailed three-pointers with a military precision. Along with tough team defense and sloppy play by the Hueytown squad, the game was a blow-out by halftime. The only question wasn't if North would win or even by how much, but if this time Mercedes would break the record for three-pointers in any Alabama high school game.

Even though they were ahead, Coach launched into a fiery half-time speech until she was interrupted by a knock on the door. Coach looked angry but motioned for Kat to open the door. Jade. Her phone hung as if by a thread in her left hand; tears ran down her face. "It's Callie," was all she said.

"She's not getting better," the doctor said. "It is only a matter of time." Jade stood on the left side of the bed, Mercedes's parents on the right. The doctor, surrounded by a sea of white faces and uniforms, stood at the foot of the bed looking like the captain of a sinking ship.

"There's nothing you can do?" Mercedes's mom asked. Or something like it. Her vocal cords were choked with tears. Her father didn't speak.

The doctor said nothing more. He handed the chart to a young face behind him. *What could this child know about death?* Mercedes wondered, but then she realized she could ask the same question of herself. Death stole childhood from everyone touched by it.

"The damage the bullet did to her brain—" the intern started. Each word stabbed Mercedes. While she wanted an answer, this wasn't the question: not how was her sister dying, but why. What led her to the perilous corner while Mercedes was drawn to the basketball court? Same parents, just three years apart. She knew the answer as clearly as she had on any calculus test: Callie had found Robert, and she had found Jade.

As the intern talked of pulling the plug, Mercedes stared at the white line threatening to flatline and the machine's red lights no longer blinking.

The doctor finally spoke again. "It's your decision." *He'd washed his hands when he entered the room*, Mercedes thought, *and he's doing it again.*

Mercedes took a step toward the bed, reached down, and touched Callie's face. Nurses, or someone, had cleared the makeup off her skin, removed her long false eyelashes, and detached the gold extensions from her hair. Callie looked more innocent than she had in years.

"Goodbye," Mercedes whispered, and she bent over to kiss her sister's forehead. It seemed cold, the shock of the sensation momentarily freezing Mercedes's quivering lips.

"I need to see it," Mercedes told Jade as they left the hospital. She wrapped her jacket tight as if to hold in the hurt in her heart. *How could one bullet*, she thought, *ruin so many lives?*

"You're sure?" Jade said. She offered her hand, but Mercedes shoved her hands deep into her pockets. The heat in the Dart didn't work. Outside a cold rain fell. "I'm not so sure if—"

"I am," Mercedes lied. She didn't know anything for sure except in a few hours her sister would be dead, and she hoped she was strong enough to "let it be" since she could not change it.

On the way, Mercedes asked Jade to stop at a craft store. Together they created a small memorial with fake flowers.

"People need to know she died here," Mercedes said as they pulled up to the corner. The rain had let up some. The wipers on the old Dart left blurry steaks. Jade parked the car.

Even in the bad weather, two people stood on the corner, wearing black hoodies. The one facing the car smoked a cigarette, and the shorter one, back to the car, rocked back and forth.

A pawn, she saw when the shorter one turned around and the streetlight hit his face, by the name of Lincoln. Mercedes pushed the passenger door open and ran toward the corner, screaming her brother's name. Jade followed quickly behind, yelling for Mercedes to stop.

Joel stepped in front of Lincoln and growled, "Stay back!" He quickly opened his jacket. Mercedes saw the gun butt sticking out from his boxers. Sister dead, brother set to die, why did she care?

"Go ahead! Shoot!" Mercedes yelled at the top of her lungs. With Jade's help, Mercedes pulled her young brother from the corner, all the while shouting, "You will not take him too!"

"I never understood this part," Jade whispered. She was one of the few acting somber. Mercedes's relatives had purged their grief at the funeral, so maybe there was nothing left in them, Mercedes figured, except room for laughter, maybe forgiveness. "How are you doing?"

Mercedes's cried-out eyes surveyed the room of long-lost relatives, old friends from the neighborhood, and every single member of her team. They were more than a team; they were family. Mercedes squeezed Jade's right arm, the "Loyalty" tattoo covered by the long sleeves of a black dress. Love and loyalty were what a person needed. It beat the false promise of the corner.

"Take as much time as you need," Coach said after expressing her condolences.

"No, I need to get out on the court if I want to get away from this." Mercedes had saved her brother, but for how long? She hadn't snitched on Robert to the police because it would do no good, but she had told her parents everything about Lincoln. She guessed that Lincoln hated her and would for some time, but one day, he'd thank her for saving his life.

"It's a light schedule the next few days. You can miss practice, even a few games if—"

"No." Mercedes shook her head, her straightened hair not moving a centimeter. She felt as out of place dressed up and made up as she would have felt resting on the bench. "I think I blew my chance with Auburn, so I need a second chance. Maybe you could call the scout?"

When Mercedes said those words, she clutched Jade's hand. For Jade, she'd been that second chance. She hoped she'd done the same for Lincoln, but it was too early to tell.

"I think with the light on you from the tournament, that won't be a problem," Coach said. "You just need to be on guard. Make sure you play your game, not the one you think she wants."

Mercedes nodded in agreement, but wouldn't smile. Not the place or the time. Today was about the past, tomorrow's game about her future. Mercedes felt stuck in between again.

Mercedes stared at the game clock telling her she had only one minute left to make two three-pointers. She didn't want to look at the nervous faces of her father and Jade in the stands, or the scowls of the opposing Huffman squad who'd hacked her hands like machetes. *It's one thing to lose*, Mercedes thought, *but another to get blown out and have a record set against you.* She wondered if she'd play—or foul—the same if she was on the other side of the court.

"Look, we've got this game," Halle said. "This is for Mercedes."

"This is for Callie," Cheryl added. Coach sat the other starters, but Halle and Cheryl insisted on coming in the last quarter because both could easily feed Mercedes the ball.

"Thanks," Mercedes said, bumping fists with her teammates as she headed out to the court. Like before a big fight at school, Mercedes felt the temperature and the tension in the building rise.

Lydia, the back-up forward, inbounded the ball to Cheryl. Cheryl quickly raced down court and found Halle open at the top of the key. Halle shot the ball out to Mercedes, who passed it right back. Halle looked confused as Mercedes cut toward the baseline. The Huffman guard pushed Mercedes hard, almost sending her out of bounds. The ref didn't call it. Mercedes moved quickly, gathered in a pass from Lydia, then used the pick set by Halle to get free. The ball sailed from her hands and bounced off the backboard and into the net to tie the record.

The home crowd exploded. Rather than getting back, North used a full-court press as Coach had instructed, even in the closing seconds, as if the score mattered. The score did not, but the scorer did. Cheryl cut off the inbound pass. A layup was hers, but she passed the ball to Lydia, who rushed it to Mercedes. The defense converged, forcing a pass to Cheryl. Cheryl tossed to Halle, who moved toward the basket, drawing in the defense. Halle passed back to Mercedes. But one second later, the ball swished through the net and fell softly back into Halle's hands.

"Foul!" Mercedes didn't like calling fouls in pickup games, but she didn't like the hurt Lincoln was putting on Jade. She needed Jade to lay the smackdown on Lincoln about the bad choices he was making. Jade had made some of the same choices. Maybe he'd listen to her.

"She moved her feet!" Lincoln shouted back. Shouting had been his only volume speaking to Mercedes ever since she pulled him off the corner. "This is bull—"

"And an odd way to celebrate non-violence," Mercedes's dad said softly. She recalled that all his yelling at Callie just drove her further away. Different child, different approach, but it didn't seem to be working. Lincoln stayed off the corner, but didn't seem part of their house. After church and a Martin Luther King celebration, they'd headed to the park to play, Lincoln against his will. Their mom rarely left home except to go to work; ever since the funeral she couldn't face the world with one less child in it.

"That MLK stuff is crap!" Lincoln said. He picked up the ball and tossed it not just off the court but into the street. Mercedes's father inhaled deeply like he'd been punched, and went to retrieve the ball. With her father's back turned, Mercedes saw Jade step forward, nose to nose with Lincoln.

"You foul me again, little man, I'll break you in half." If Mercedes's father wouldn't be tough, Mercedes knew Jade would be. Jade got up in Lincoln's face. "You think you're real tough, don't you?"

"Stop spitting on me," Lincoln shot back. Mercedes grabbed Jade, but she pulled away. Jade ripped off her long-sleeved maroon shirt, down to a white beater. Lincoln's eyes grew wide.

"Get your eyes here." Jade pointed at the "Loyalty" tattoo on her right arm. "You think you know what you're getting into with goons like Robert, but trust me, you know nothing."

Lincoln laughed, but stopped when Jade grabbed his right arm and twisted it behind his back. "You're hurting me," Lincoln whined like the little kid Mercedes guessed he was inside.

"You don't know hurt!" Jade shouted into his ear and she wrenched his arm tighter. "How much do you think Callie hurt when that bullet went into her skull? How much do you think your sister and parents hurt watching her lie there dying, kept alive by machines? How much—"

"I don't know, let me go!" Mercedes stood in front of the two to obstruct her dad's view.

"So what are you gonna do, act all tough, be on the corner, be somebody?"

Lincoln started to speak but stopped when Jade wrapped her other arm tight around his throat. He tried to pry her arm away without success. "This is what dying feels like. This is what standing always on guard feels like. This is life on that corner. It is nothing but a stranglehold."

"I can't breathe," Lincoln muttered.

"That's right, you can't and here's why." Mercedes felt her heart drop as Jade told her brother stories about gang life, about what she did to get in, what she did to get out. Mercedes didn't know how much was true and was afraid to ask. She sensed Lincoln was afraid too.

"So I've been there, like when my pops died," Jade said, twisting Lincoln's arm tighter until tears formed in his eyes. "Angry and scared. I was acting more like a wolf than a person."

"That's enough," Mercedes said, placing her hand on Jade's arm.

"There's an old Cherokee story that we have two wolves inside us. Lincoln, you have a bad wolf roaring inside you so loud you can't hear. But you know what, little man? You have a good one too, like your sister," Jade said. "She's that good wolf living in you."

Jade released Lincoln. He stumbled and

fell to the ground. Mercedes and Jade offered their hands to help him. He waved them away, cleared the tears from his eyes, and coughed. Jade turned and kissed Mercedes.

"And do you know which one wins?" Jade continued.

"Which one?" Lincoln asked as he brushed off his dirty pants.

"The one you feed."

"Mercedes, in my office," Coach said as she walked out onto the court for practice.

"That doesn't sound good," Cheryl said. Mercedes couldn't tell from Cheryl's tone if she was concerned or just busting her. "That's worse than getting called into the principal's office."

Mercedes put her head down and jogged to the office, but Coach stayed on the court, starting practice. When Mercedes opened the office door she saw Tina Franklin seated at the desk.

"Sit down, Mercedes." Tina pointed to the other open chair in front of Coach's desk. Mercedes tried not to let on how surprised she was to see the Auburn recruiter. "I heard about your last game and that you set the record for three-pointers in an Alabama high school game."

Mercedes beamed with pride, but the smile left as Franklin's frown filled the room.

"We don't need record setters at Auburn," Franklin said. She tapped her left foot against the floor as she spoke. "We don't need shooters, passers, or rebounders. We need players."

"That's me." Mercedes started to explain how Coach wanted her to set the record.

"Your coach explained that to me." Franklin's voice dropped to almost a whisper. "She also told me about your sister. I'm sorry. She said she thought setting that record was something you needed after what just happened, but trust me, Mercedes, I've seen too many girls like you trying to fill the holes in their hearts. Dead brothers, fathers, sisters, mothers, cousins. Death is selfish; it never gives back."

Images of Callie's funeral flashed through Mercedes's head on fast-forward. "I know."

"No matter how many threes you shoot, it never really works."

Mercedes's head bobbed up and down like her mom's did in church. "So while I know that nothing can fill that hole in your heart, I hope this will help." Franklin handed Mercedes a single sheet of paper. On the top of it was the Auburn logo, on the bottom a place for a signature, and in between the words that made Mercedes's broken but healing heart soar: "Letter of Intent."

## ABOUT THE AUTHOR

Patrick Jones is a former librarian for teenagers. He received lifetime achievement awards from the American Library Association and the Catholic Library Association in 2006. Jones has authored several titles for the following Darby Creek series: Turbocharged (2013); Opportunity (2013); The Dojo (2013), which won the YALSA Quick Picks for Reluctant Young Adult Readers award; The Red Zone (2014); The Alternative (2014); Bareknuckle (2014); and Locked Out (2015). He also authored *The Main Event: The Moves and Muscle of Pro Wrestling* (2013), which received the Chicago Public Library's Best of the Best Books list. While Patrick lives in Minneapolis, he still considers Flint, Michigan, his home. He can be found on the web at www.connectingya.com.